JOSEY'S HILLBILLY HEAVEN

Based on a true story!

Bev Beck

Mouse Gate Series

Mouse Gate Press
1103 Middlecreek
Friendswood, Texas 77546
281-992-3131 TEL
www.MouseGate.com

ISBN: 978-1-64883-0921
USB: 6-43977-40921-8
FIRST EDITION
1 2 3 4 5 6 7 8 9 10

This book is dedicated to Dorothy and Jim,
my mom and dad.

About the Author

Bev Jo Beck, also known as Josey, was born in St. Louis Missouri. She grew up in the foothills along with her brothers and sisters. She knew the hunger and the pain of having very little. There were hard times and there were good times.

She learned to work the earth and make things grow. She loved it! She was close to God and nature. Her experience and curiosity of the big world around her taught her how to survive. Her children around her were the root of her happiness. She helped others and in turn helped herself.

About the Book

Josey's Hillbilly Heaven is based on some truth, some fiction, with twist and turns to create some fun for her readers. Josey's experience growing up in the hills of Missouri helped set her standards and beliefs in her life and loves for a solid foundation of the person she is today.

Her book Hillbilly Heaven will let you know what a strong-willed youngster she was and the strong adult she is today.

Chapter 1

Josey stood at her kitchen sink doing something she never imagined. Washing trash! What a concept. The recycle truck would be at the curb in front of her house early the next morning. She was not going to put out dirty cans and bottles for them to pick up. No Way! Glass in one box, plastic in another, and cans in another. Newspaper and cardboard were put in bags. She wasn't washing these things like she did her dishes. She just rinsed and dried them enough to say they weren't sticky and messy, tearing off the labels.

Josey stretched up on her toes, looking out her window. The children in the neighborhood had all gone inside and it was starting to get dark. Josey had spent most of the day at the hospital.

She had met her friend Ruby just three months earlier. Ruby was a very outspoken and to the point person. She wasn't rude, she just said things exactly the way they were. To Josey, that showed honesty.

Ruby taught third grade at Ashton Elementary, just a few blocks away. Her students loved her and often brought her gifts. They called her Miss Ruby. One morning a student named Michael brought her a beautiful opal ring. She asked him where he had gotten it. "From his mother," he had told her.

Ruby called his mother. He had taken it from her jewelry box. It had once belonged to his grandmother. Ruby didn't want to get the boy in trouble, but she knew it had to be returned. Ruby and Michael's mother became friends.

Miss Ruby laid in her hospital bed in a coma breathing from a ventilator tube. Josey remembered sitting in the waiting room the first time she had taken her to the hospital emergency.

"Josey, I think I have to go to the hospital!" It was Ruby on the phone, "Josey I fell, and I need help."

Josey dropped the pants she was hemming and took her friend to the hospital. The nurse took Ruby into a room while Josey waited. When the doctor came out, Josey hurried in. Ruby looked so pale and frightened.

"What is happening to me? Do I have to stay here," She asked?

"For now," Josey told her.

Ruby was admitted and dialysis started the next day. She was a diabetic and blood sugars bounced up and down. Her kidneys failed her; her hands and feet were swollen. After three days of dialysis, Ruby started feeling better. She was sent to a medical care facility for rehabilitation. There was hope. The rehab, along with dialysis seemed to be working.

One night while Ruby slept, her sugar had dropped,

and she was rushed to the hospital again. She had a stroke this time. For three days Miss Ruby lay in her bed with her niece Pat, Pat's husband Rick, and Josey by her side. Watching her every breathe, they prayed for her recovery and looking for the slightest movements.

She never woke up.

Tears ran down Josey's face, remembering that long, hot day. Her hands shook. A sharp pain ran through her thumb and blood started oozing warm and sticky. The sharp edge of the can that she was rinsing had cut into her. Grabbing a paper towel, she wrapped her thumb and sat down. "this isn't right," she cried out, "This just isn't right!" She needed more time to know her friend.

The stainless-steel tea kettle whistled loud and shrill. Josey poured the boiling water over her tea bag in her cup. Drinking her green tea, she thought of the mornings when her and Ruby would have tea and conversation.

Miss Ruby was a child of Mexico. Her mother was Inca Indian. She was a tiny lady with long black hair that was kept in braid. Her father was Mexican. He was a stern man who took care of his wife and children.

Ruby talked a lot about her family. They had big dinners with chicken, rice, beans, and a lot of tortillas. She loved her brothers and sisters very much and she missed them.

She often talked about her Bible. She spent lots of time reading from the good book. However, she was very confused about life. It sometimes can be very confusing.

The clock chimed twelve times. Josey was tired. As tired as she was, she just wasn't ready to sleep. When she did go to bed, she felt like she couldn't sleep. She was an exceptionally light sleeper; this came from self-training and listening for sounds in the night. Josey often sat on her porch swing late into the evening after the children went to bed.

Re-runs were on tv. Josey remembered re-runs of Gilligan's Island over and over. She did not mind it back then. It was something to watch with a bowl of popcorn. Not too many channels back then to fight over, she thought. Her and her brothers were just glad to have something to watch. The good old black and white.

Josey sat there remembering when her own father passed away. She took care of him in her home on Grand Avenue. He was a strong man who lived a very rough life. He was stocky with big, thick glasses, and he liked his whiskey. He was a brick layer in St. Louis, Missouri for a time.

Josey remembered only one disagreement with her dad. He and her mom had been divorced for quite some time, but always remained friends. He still came to see her nearly every day. They had both remarried. Her dad and his new wife, Euleta, stood in her mother's kitchen arguing late one night. Her mother had already gone to bed.

Josey's brother Bobby had found a stray dog running loose in the street in front of the house. It was a hot night and Bobby brought the dog in to give him water. The little dog walked up to Euleta, raised his right hind leg, and pissed down her cast on her broken left foot. She started screaming and hopping around bumping into the table and knocking over chairs.

"Get that damn dog out here," she yelled.

Bobby just stood at the other side of the kitchen laughing. Josey came out of the living room and looked at her dad and then at Euleta.

"Don't come into my mother's house yelling at anyone here. You and dad can get the hell out of my mother's house and do your damn fighting outside!" I told it to them straight faced.

The next morning Josey looked out the kitchen window. The sun was just coming up. She couldn't believe what she saw. Her dad and Euleta were standing in the middle of the yard still fighting and yelling at each other.

Ain't love just wonderful. "Get married again dad," she yelled out the door, "you two go home." She always loved her dad; no matter what he did or where he went.

As hospice came to Josey's door with oxygen, her dad had taken his last breath. Her father had been fighting cancer for some time. It had finally taken its toll.

Josey had been diagnosed with cancer herself just a few years before. Her mom and dad came to Michigan to be with her. Josey had surgery with her mother and father by her side. She fought cancer several times. She came through it all and raised her six children to be adults.

Josey sat on her swing slowly falling asleep. The night air was peaceful. Just before daybreak, Josey woke up with a pain in her back. That porch swing seat was not the ideal place to fall asleep. Funny how she could fall asleep on that hard swing, but trying to sleep in her warm, cozy waterbed was a chore. She could sleep on the hard wood on their porch growing up in the woods in Missouri. The outdoor air was so warm and breezy.

"Jo are you awake? Where are you?"

The big brown rooster would crow, and Josey would stretch and yawn to a new morning. Her sister Helen was loudly snoring. The boys were doing chores before school. Josey often thought about her childhood; how different things were back then. The hairstyles, clothes, and even shoes were different. Josey liked the black and white oxfords and old buster browns.

The women's hair was different too. The hair was cut short in the front and the sides, while the back was long. The best of both worlds.

On really hot days, Josey kept her hair in a ponytail. The front was kept short and the back was pulled up so that it didn't get in the way while working in the fields.

Chapter 2

The sun shone hot while working in the cotton fields. Josey's little brother, Clayton and little sister, Helen were leaning over working and sweating ahead of her. She was in charge of the younger kids even while working in the fields.

Clayton picked up a little green snake and threw it at Helen, she started screaming. The snake had landed across her left shoulder and she couldn't shake it off. Here comes Uncle Carl.

"What are you two doing? Your supposed to be working. Knock that shit off and git back to work. Josey aren't you watching them two?'

"I was," said Josey.

"Well, you all get back to work and stop the horseshit," scowled Uncle Carl.

After her uncle went back down the long white row of cotton, Josey thought to herself, "well I certainly don't see any horseshit flying. What is he talking about?" He sat on his cotton sack smoking one of those big, nasty cigars watching the kids work. He took a big drink of lemonade and started coughing and choking. Now that, to Josey, was the horseshit.

The rows of the tomatoes heavy on the vines meant

canning season was here. Josey and her Aunt Inez canned tomatoes, green beans, and pickles. The corn was cut off the cob and frozen.

Uncle Carl took Josey and the boys into the neighboring corn fields at night. They came home with big, black bags full of corn. Josey sat with a big knife cutting off kernels and putting them in plastic bags to freeze. Uncle Carl told her to always put the corn on the table while cutting down into it.

Josey's hands and arms were tired. She took a cob full of corn and decided she could do it on her lap. She was confident that her uncle didn't know anything. Afterall, he was full of horseshit. Down came the knife! Blood ran as the knife slipped and went into her knee.

She grabbed a towel and held it while her uncle slapped her in the back of the head. The cut was about two inches long. Josey could still see the scar. One night they went into a huge corn field. The field corn was to feed the animals.

"Shit," Carl said, "this is damn field corn. We will boil some up and save the rest for the chickens."

Josey bit into the corn and it was pretty chewy. It took a lot of chewing, but they ate it. Not too bad when washed down with cold water.

The tomatoes were Josey's favorite. She liked helping Aunt Inez can them. She could slip chunks of warm tomato in her mouth while peeling them. They were put in hot pans of water then cooled down. The skins would come right off. The peas were popped out of the pods and put into bags to freeze. It was all good come winter.

For a time, they all lived in an old farmhouse surrounded by peach trees. It was called Peach Orchard. Josey felt like she was in heaven. Talk about being full of something; when the peaches were ripe Josey ate them every day. She didn't care if she had anything else, except tomatoes of course.

Josey always washed the jars and peeled the peaches while they were still hot, out of the pan. She didn't care. She would always steal a big warm chunk of peach. It was indescribable.

"I wonder if there is anyone that doesn't like peaches," she thought, how could there be?"

The hot peach cobbler in the wintertime was worth all the work. Sometimes there was homemade ice cream to go with it. The pudding to make the ice cream was cooked over low heat, then put in metal ice trays with dividers taken out. They were put in the freezer. It had to be stirred several times during freezing. When there was nice big snow, ice cream was made from the biggest pile of snow there was.

The pudding was made, then cooled. It was made of sugar, vanilla, egg yolks, and cream. Then it was mixed with snow. Snow ice cream was believed to have begun around 500 BC. During the fifth century BC, ancient Greeks ate snow mixed with honey and fruit.

Hippocrates encouraged his antient Greek patients to eat ice, as it livened the life juices and encouraged well-being. The Roman emperor, Nero 37-68 AD had ice brought to him from the mountains and added it with fruits.

Ice cream recipes first appeared in England in the eighteenth century. The first recipe for it was published in Mrs. Mary Eales recipes in London in 1718. Ice cream became inexpensive for everyone in the mid eighteenth century.

The first cone recipe was made and published by Mrs. A. B. Marshall's book of cooking in 1888. The cone was popularized in the U.S. at the world's fair in St. Louis, Missouri in 1904. The place where Josey was born, St. Louis, Missouri city hospital. It became popular throughout the world in the second half of the twentieth century after cheap refrigeration became common.

Josey made the snow ice cream for her own children and she taught them how to make it. She made recipe books for each of her six children with all the favorite family recipes she grew up with. Home-made mayonnaise cake was always a hit at the holidays. Her mother, grandmother, and aunts never measured anything. They just knew what to do!

When Josey got older, she re-experimented with the recipes so she could perfect them for her children. She mixed and measured ingredients until she got them just right and wrote them down. The chocolate gravy was tricky. When it started cooking and got really hot it would turn into big lumps and eventually would smooth out into smooth, silky chocolate gravy.

Josey wasn't sure if the saying about carrots making your eyes better was true, but she ate them a lot. She also cooked them often for her children. When she couldn't get them to eat vegetables, she would put them in a blender and mix them into sauces. Sometimes she didn't like doing that, but she wanted her children to be healthy. She did not have much money for doctors, so she did all the things she knew was good for them.

When the children had colds, she would take advice from an old family doctor and it seemed to work. She would get a big bag of plain, salty potato chips and room temperature coke. The salt from the potato chips would help the swelling in their throat and the warm coke would wash it all down and settle their stomach. Kids will eat potato chips and drink even when they are sick and won't eat anything else. Josey even does that for her grandchildren.

Chapter 3

Friends like Ruby came once in a lifetime. Josey had lots of friends through the years that she loved and missed, but Ruby was different. She was a deep thinker and loved her God and loved her life. How unfair it was to lose her friendship like that. But that's God's choice. He is the big guy.

Josey's kids were all grown with families of their own. Grandchildren are so great. God does some awesome stuff. Sometimes things we don't understand too. It is the way it is. The morning started out so nice and beautiful.

The trailer park where Josey lived later was nice and peaceful most of the time. Josey didn't neighbor too much. Some of the neighbors were real characters. She loved to see the kids running in yards, chasing whatever; sometimes each other. Her big porch didn't have a swing, but it had big benches all around it.

With the hot sun and the storms that Michigan weather is made of, especially in the winter, it all had to be painted, which Josey did herself. Working alone was always her way to go. No talk, just work. Her own thoughts kept her happy.

Her son, Billy her only son, was always busy. He

worked, even when he was in school. He cleaned the bathrooms after school every day. He gave his mother money from every pay and gave her money for him to save. He delivered papers and also worked in a shop.

He eventually got married and had children of his own: Robert, Christopher, and Nicky, who eventually gave him grandchildren. He still always made Josey a priority in his life. They were buddies. Mother and son!

Billy was also born in St. Louis, Missouri, at the same hospital Josey was born in. His dad was born in Missouri too, Kennett, Missouri. He was a dishwasher in Poplar Bluff where he and Josey were married. His father later worked in General Motors in Flint, Michigan.

Debbie Sue, Billy's sister was born in Flint, MI, a beautiful baby girl. Billy loved her as he did all of his sisters yet to come. Debbie Sue was his first playmate. He would cover her up at night. He was only three, but he helped keep her safe. Debbie Sue grew up to have beautiful daughters of her own. Very sweet and honest loving girls.

Josey's daughter Sarah Jane was a different child. She had speech disability and learning disability which she overcame. She now is very computer smart, which Josey was not. She didn't have time or patience for it. She played around with it some but will never be as good as Sarah Jane.

Josey later became a writer, but still could not master

that damn computer of hers. Josey and her kids' father later divorced. The dream of being married once to one great guy was shattered. Life can play tricks on you. Every time you think you mastered it, you hit a pothole.

Josey's way of dealing with life is to say, "Oh well, I will daydream a bit and just start over." That always works for her. She doesn't always like change, but it is sometimes good and exciting. A new day, a new challenge!

The loss of Ruby a good friend and a kind soul, was just another life experience that changed Josey. Every bad thing in her life helped change her and to make her appreciate life itself. Rough will make you tough! Getting hit with something tough can only make you smarter. Pain is definitely a wake-up call.

After Ruby passed, her niece Pat and Pat's husband did some fundraisers for her funeral expenses. Josey made a special candle and named it after her. She sold them to help with expenses and made some for her family. It was another thing she could do by herself. She made up different candles for people that she cared about. Mixing different scents was fun. Creating her own scents and names for them.

She sold them in a consignment store and in flea markets. She experimented with the colors too making them her own. She only used Golden Soy Wax. It seemed to work the best for her.

Josey remembered going down to Ruby's place and

taking her two little poodles out for her when she got sick. She would go clean up her yard every few days and mow it too. One day when she went to go clean up her little dog's forget-me-nots that they left in the yard Josey was surprised. She said, "Ruby has someone else been cleaning up the dog mess in the yard for you?" Ruby started laughing. She said she looked out the window and the squirrels were eating the dog's poop out of the yard.

Josey said, "well the next time you see them, you thank them for me." They both had a good laugh. Josey didn't know squirrels did that.

Josey's dream of being somebody was already a reality. She was Josey, a daughter, a mother, a grandmother, and eventually great-grandmother. She was special after all, God made her too!

She was a butcher, baker, and a candle maker. Her dream of being a writer finally came true. She was somebody. Everyone is, in their own right.

Her grandchildren were a special joy to her. The first word Josey taught them was lardass. They would laugh and say it with her. Eventually they learned to talk more, those words didn't matter to them. It just gave them a good start in being interested in the English language. They couldn't say any other swear words, only lardass. It was funny and easy for them to say.

Chapter 4

One morning Josey was walking her big dog Ben, when someone yelled, "hey, don't bring that dog in my yard!" Josey looked up to see a neighbor lady standing by her own trailer yelling.

"What the hell," thought Josey. She never let Ben leave a big steamy pile, which he was very capable of, in anyone else's yard. She was careful not to let him do that. She always carried pick up bags.

Josey screamed out, "he's not in your yard!"

The lady yelled back, "well don't bring him over here." Josey was getting pretty mad at this rude wench who thought she had trailer park authority.

"Well, I pay rent too, and he's not in your yard so crawl back in your hole Bitch and shut your mouth," yelled Josey. Well, that was the end of that! Josey went to the manager's office and told them what happened. She did not let people intimidate her if she knew she was in the right. She didn't like trouble., but she didn't let it run her either.

Ben was a big, white fluffy Great Pyrenees and as stubborn as Josey. He was a beautiful dog and all the kids loved him. Josey's little dog Sally Mae was a cute chubby Puggle. She was Pug and Beagle mixed. Those dogs should never have been bred, but they did make them a breed of their own. Sally Mae had trouble with her eyes, ears, and she had two rows of teeth. She was so funny, and she was beautiful to Josey. Her daughter, Lisa had got her for a gift.

Josey remembered the pets she had growing up in Missouri. A big white rabbit she had found in the yard beside her old farmhouse and brought in. That rabbit would watch television and eat popcorn or ice cream with the kids. Their aunt named him Napoleon. It followed Josey everywhere. Then it started chewing holes in the blankets and rugs. Aunt Inez put him back outside and it ran away.

Eventually, they got a big black dog named Rocky. The boys all ran with him playing and throwing balls for him. He kept those little rascals busy. They also had goats in the yard until one took a biscuit right out of her aunt's hand. Josey didn't know what happened to the goats but one day they were gone.

One afternoon, after having bean soup for lunch, the boys decided to fill the big metal tub out back with water. They were going to get in it and play motorboat. Silly boys! The dog decided he wanted to get in with them. What a mess. The dog got a good bath, right along with the boys.

One day they decided to take the dog for a walk. Up the side trail they went. Eventually they ran into a couple of bigger boys who wanted trouble. They turned the dog loose and told him to "go get 'em!" That stupid dog just took off running away up the hill. The big boys started laughing. They eventually made friends and the damn dog never did come back.

Josey loved animals. She could talk to them, but they couldn't talk back. She liked that. To her, there was nothing better than to cuddle with an animal.

Josey decided to let Ben run a little bit. She thought she could keep up if he ran slow. Well guess what? He took off and down she went. She didn't want to let go of the leash and lose her dog. He was a runner much to her surprise. She found that out the hard way. She got a firsthand tour of the park personally. She got to feel the grass and rocks up close and personal. He had no mercy.

About a week later, her friend Wendy came over and wanted to walk Ben. Josey told her, "do not let him run!" Well Wendy decided she could handle it. Off they went Wendy hit the ground, full face. Josey stood there watching. What could she do?

When the dog finally stopped, Wendy got up. "Damn, that dog can run," she said. Well Josey decided it was time to take him to the dog park for runs. It was fenced in and he could run like the wind. More like a tornado.

Little Sally Mae was a small dog. Fat but close to the ground. She thought she was as big as any of them. Josey took her to the dog park. She would put her in the smaller fenced in area. She would start fights with the other dogs. Even the big ones.

Josey would always say to her, "you can't run with the big dogs Sally Mae, you have to stay on the porch."

Josey had another good friend, Carlene. She was Josey's lunch buddy. They went out to lunch quite often. Carlene would pick Josey up sometimes and they would go for fish dinners. On holidays, they would go have a steak. Sometimes Wendy would go with them for coffee and doughnuts. Josey was mostly a loner, but she cared about her friends and did spend time with them.

Back home in Poplar Bluff, Missouri Josey's friends Suzie and Linda were raising their own families. She lost track of Linda but kept in touch with Suzie. She was later married to Suzie's brother Dennis. They married in Michigan where Dennis later passed away.

Josey was not a stranger to death. She worked in a nursing home where she was a nurse aid. Death is never easy. Especially when you see it happen firsthand. It is horrible to have to say goodbye to someone for the last time. She never got used to it but learned how to accept it.

Josey loved life and that's what she wanted to see. Babies being born. New plants flowering. Tomatoes ripening. The hot Missouri sun with a big icy glass of lemonade and sitting with a friend watching things grow was her heaven.

It was peaceful seeing God's work and trying to understand it all. She would watch the bugs, butterflies, and birds wander about. How beautiful they were. Well, some bugs weren't so cute, but they were special in their own way.

"Some bugs are mean," she thought. They sting and they bite, and she never knew quite why they did that. How do they all start out so different? God made everything even the mean ugly bugs. With all of the wonderful things in the world that He made, He sure had to be busy for a long time.

Chapter 5

Working in the nursing home was quite the experience for Josey. Death and taxes and Josey getting into trouble was a sure thing. She made a wonderfully different type of friends while working there. The history behind some of these elderly people was amazing. She met a lady that came from Germany. Her name was Elizabeth. She told Josey stories from her childhood. She had seen Hitler when she was a small child. She remembered running for home when the noise of the bombs hit. Her mother calling out for her, grabbing her, and running to the house. She was writing a book about it all.

Real chocolates were sent to her by her family in Germany. She sometimes would share them with Josey. They would often send her newspapers from there. That was really something.

Josey got a German Shepherd puppy and asked Elizabeth to give her a real German name for a dog. She named him Hasso. Josey had her favorite even though she wouldn't say it. Another lady she spent extra time with was Mary.

Mary was a sad and lonely little lady who mostly wanted to be by herself. Well, Josey quickly changed that.

One afternoon while pushing Mary from the dining room she, of course, had one of her clumsy mishaps. She was pushing Mary in her wheelchair down the long hall back to her room just singing away to Mary, and down she went. Mary turned and looked at her laying on the floor.

"What happened Josey?" she asked.

Out came the head nurse from her office, "Josey, what is going on out here?"

"Well, I don't know," she said looking up at the nurse who was standing with her hands on her hips. "I slipped and fell," said Josey.

The nurse looked down the long hall behind her. "Oh My!" she said. For what seemed like a mile back was yellow steamy splats all along the floor in a perfect row.

"What is that?" the nurse asked looking down at Josey.

"Well, I don't know," she said. Josey looked up at Mary and she was looking like she was going to cry. The yellow blobs were oozing from Mary's chair. Josey looked back at the nurse who was helping her up.

"I guess I was following the yellow brick road and slipped on a brick," she replied jokingly. The nurse shook her head and went back into her office shutting the door behind her. Mary started laughing.

"I am sorry Josey," she said.

Josey told her, "we are in it for the long haul." They both laughed and Mary felt better. Josey pushed her into her room and told her she would be right back. She got a mop and bucket and lots of paper towels and cleaned the floor. She went back to Mary's room and gave her a shower. After she got Mary cleaned up and settled in front of the television, she took a shower herself. For the rest of the day, she had to work in hospital pajamas.

Josey remembered when the Berlin wall was brought down. She sat in Elizabeth's room and watched the news with her. Elizabeth was so overwhelmed with the changing history, she cried.

It was a happy cry.

The next afternoon Josey pushed several of the residents into the dining room to their tables. Mary asked her what they were having for supper.

"What are we having?" they all asked.

"Well," Josey said. "We are supposed to have monkey stew, but the monkey got away. They couldn't catch it." Everyone laughed and had a good time talking about what would go into the monkey stew. Here comes the nurse to see what Josey was up to now.

She stood in the doorway with her hands on her hips looking at everyone. They all got quiet. She shook her head and away she went. Everyone had a smile on their face, Josey was in trouble again. She thought to herself, some of these people are mothers, fathers, and grandparents who had jobs, cars, and homes of their own at one time. Life sure changes and does go on generation after generation.

Chapter 6

Working in the nursing home opened up two different worlds for Josey. She had her children to come home to after a long day of working with the elderly. After resting and talking with her kids she would make dinner, do laundry, and get things ready for the next day.

Raising children and working is very hard, but Josey didn't mind it. She loved coming home every day to her kids waiting for her. To see their smiles as she came in, was worth it all. The children grew and life went on. They soon had families of their own. The grandbabies made life warm and wonderful.

Josey spent time with her friends talking about work and everyday life. She was invited to a birthday party one hot July afternoon for the husband of a friend and co-worker.

Bea had worked with Josey, along with friends, Wendy and Carlene. Everything was nice and her friends were all talking and laughing. A sudden strange feeling came over Josey. Something was wrong.

She took off down the long hall towards the bathroom. Her head was swirling and she almost fainted as she leaned against the wall. She looked for a water fountain, but there wasn't one. She felt like she had choked on a big gulp of water. She heard her son's voice calling her, "Mom…..mommy!"

"I have to call home," she thought to herself. What is wrong? She told her friend Wendy that she had to get home.

"Something is wrong," Josey said. She drove home in a daze. When she got home, Teresa was on the phone with the hospital emergency room where she worked. Josey's son Billy had drowned!

Josey was in shock. She couldn't speak. She was frozen. Teresa was supposed to be headed to work at the emergency department where Billy was taken. She drove Josey to the hospital in tears. She was talking to the doctor. He told her that her brother was gone. He didn't make it. Teresa pulled the car over and started screaming in tears. She needed a minute to gain her composure so she could drive to the hospital.

Josey was heartbroken, she couldn't cry, she couldn't speak, she couldn't think. This isn't real. Its not happening, is all that went through her mind. Her son was in his forties and he was a good swimmer. He took lifeguard lessons and his yearbook even said he was a good swimmer. How could this be?

Josey slowly walked into the room where her son lay. He didn't look at her and smile like he always did. He laid there cold and blue. Josey stood over him holding his hand and waiting for that smile that never came.

Tears started running down her face. She couldn't breathe. There was no place to run and hide and stop all of this. It was real. To lose someone to death is devastating. The loss of a parent, spouse, a relative, or a friend is very difficult; not less important but different. Somehow the loss of a child, her child, is almost intolerable. It was and is still hard for Josey to talk about or even accept. The only way to describe it is like when she saw kids out playing and wondered where her child is. Always looking for him to come around a corner or through a door.

It is like that still. She is always looking for him or waiting for the phone to ring to hear his voice. That feeling never seems to go away, ever. He should be here with her always. Her mind would not stop waiting for him, waiting to hear from him. Every day is like that for her.

To cry is to admit defeat. That would mean it is over, for her, it will never be over. She has found a way to keep her son with her forever. She thanks God for showing her how to do that, and how to never give up on anything she cares about. Like her son, her baby boy, Billy Lee. He will never leave her. He is in her heart and soul. She thanks God every day for giving him to her and letting her have him in her life.

There is nothing as deep and meaningful and lonely as a mother's cry. It is very hard to get through it. To know that she must keep going on with life for the rest of her children who she loves just as much. Five beautiful and strong girls. There is no medicine for pain so deep. She didn't want medicine for pain. She wanted to remember everything about him. His laughter, his cries, his anger, and his love. She didn't want this memory cheated or clouded.

She was not angry with God! How could she be? He only took back what was his to start with. She wanted to sleep, just to see him in her dreams. She could go back and hold her baby again. Billy Lee is in her heart, curled up in a little corner of his own. She carries him with her everywhere she goes. He is always with her. Her son, her only son, her favorite son!

Chapter 7

When Josie left her home in Missouri, she hoped to find new beginnings.

She left her mom, her dad, brothers, sisters, aunts, uncles, and cousins. She did not like to travel. It was going into the unknown. Her husband wanted to work at the General Motors factory in Flint, Michigan. The move was good, and he had family there. He wanted to be able to support his own new family.

Michigan was cold and lonely. The people there were very different. Josey soon adjusted. She cried for her family she left, but she was making her own family. She often thinks of all of her cousins that she grew up with.

Running through the cornfields under the stars and catching fireflies was still in her dreams at night. Climbing up into the tall trees was a freedom that she left behind.

Being a wife and mother was new and scary. She wanted to do this but leaving her childhood behind was hard. Sometimes it wasn't good, but she survived it and grew stronger for it. Her hillbilly heaven wasn't always heaven, but she held on to the memories of sitting in the hot sun surrounded by big red tomatoes, green beans, and corn.

Running under the moonlight, stars, and chasing the fireflies was behind her. When she first came to Michigan her nights were long and full of tears. She eventually got used to the changes from childhood to motherhood.

New adventures awaited her and her children to come. The telephone calls were short and sweet and very expensive. The first time she went to Missouri to visit her family was a little rough. She had to take the bus with her son, Billy Lee and her two little daughters, Debbie Sue and Sarah Jane. Sarah was only a few months old and Billy and Debbie were toddlers.

She had a baby harness for Billy and had to juggle the girls. The trips got fewer. The money was tight. She did visit her family as often as she could. Michigan winters seemed to get longer and colder. She eventually had three more daughters: Lisa, Sheila, and Teresa.

As time went on her family got bigger. There were grandchildren and great grandchildren that kept her busy. Josey always wanted to be a teacher. Now she has a classroom all of her own full of beautiful kids to teach about life and love.

Josey canned tomatoes, made jellies, and grew her own little garden in the back of her house on Grand Avenue. She made some of her children's clothes and toys. She taught them how to sew and cook for their families.

She made her own hillbilly heaven right there in Michigan. Oh yes, she still daydreams about anything and everything. Sitting in front of the television, she watches re-runs of Gilligan's Island, unbelievable. The old big black and white tv. turned into a big flatscreen color television.

Her own children watch some of the same episodes as she did with her brothers and sisters; some in color some in black and white. Life seems to speed by in a whirl. It really does go round and round.

Josey now sees her cousins that she grew up with on her computer and on Facebook. They are like strangers to her now, but some how she feels like she still misses them and loves them as she did when they were children playing in the yard. She sees herself sitting on the floor playing jacks and I-

spy with them. She will always remember the fighting and the hugging.

Childhood memories are personal and special, but not always something you can talk about. She wanted to hug her cousins, aunts, and uncles once more. Instead, she just looks on her computer and sees their familiar faces and thinks about them. She wonders if they even think of her. She checks her computer screen and sees her cousins and their families. The children she will always love and never get to know.

Chapter 8

Listening to oldies on music choice tv, Josey remembered the old sugar shack. It was a place where Josey and her friend Suzy would go to dance to the juke box and have sodas. She loved her pink poodle skirt. She wore it with a flared tulle cancan. She had a black one and a pink one that actually was itchy and uncomfortable. They were fun to wear with her black and white oxfords and bobby socks that had a twist to them.

Cashmere sweaters that were buttoned down the back was soft and had her initial on them. A big letter J was on the front. She wore her hair in a ponytail that was tied up with a little scarf that hung down. Her and Suzy would make up dances that they could do there.

The sugar shack was a comfort place on Saturdays after going to school all week. A place to meet new friends. When Suzy passed away Josey felt a big loss. She hadn't seen Suzy in a few years, and she missed the times she spent with her. Now she sees Suzy's son on Facebook and thinks of the times when her and Suzy took her own son, Billy Lee to the movies.

Billy was only about two years old and full of fun. Josey would dress him up in little boots and outfits that was fashion that the Beatles wore. They were a new and upcoming band from England that appeared on the Ed Sullivan show. They called him their little Beatle. He had a Beatle haircut too.

When Billy's dad was at work Josey and Suzy took Billy to the movies and to the park often. Once, when they were at the movies, Billy stood up in his seat and was looking at the guy behind him. He started reaching out and calling him daddy. He started crying and trying to climb over the seat to get him. The guy didn't know what to say. They had to leave in the middle of the movie.

Josey would take Billy to K-Mart and sit on the floor with him and play with the wind-up toys. She would let him pick one to take home. His first words were "go K-Mart".

The road to Michigan was long, tiresome, and emotional. Josey wanted to be a writer but that came later. She wrote little stories and tucked them away thinking, "someday!" The children's stories came easy. Her children inspired her and gave her lots of wonderful ideas. To sit and just watch children play is so sweet and unpredictable. They have such amazingly new ideas about life and how things should and could be. They would often make someone's underwear go up their ass by saying something unexpected. When they were small, life was still new and fresh to them. They wonder and they learn and express their knowledge in new ways. Josey missed watching her kids grow and experience new things as children.

Debbie now has two girls. Beautiful, awesome daughters and they are now experiencing motherhood. My how time goes by. Billy Lee has a girl, two boys, and is a grandpa. Lisa has two boys and a sweet daughter. The boys look just like their dad. She is now a grandmother. Sheila has three wonderful daughters. Teresa has a pretty freckle faced girl and a handsome boy.

Josey can't believe the grandchildren are starting to drive. She says her grandchildren are getting older than her. She didn't drive until she was in her twenties. Her husband had a gallbladder attack, and she went with him to the hospital in Flint. He had to have surgery so he told her she would have to drive herself home. She had never drove before.

They had a 1967 Volkswagen. She actually got in the car and decided that she can do this! Well…she bucked that damn car all the way home just guessing what gear to shift in for what speed. She didn't have a clue what she was doing. It was scary, exciting, and fun.

She drove back and forth to the hospital and eventually learned how to drive that damn car. She didn't really know the rules of the road, but she made up her own. She was speeding one night going home and here comes a cop. The lights and sirens scared the hell out of her. She didn't want to stop and be in trouble so she decided she could outrun him. She wanted to get home to her son who was with the sitter.

She stepped on the gas ad flew through yards between houses thinking, "oh, I hope the hell there are no fences." She got lucky and lost him and finally got back on a road to home. Her heart was pounding, and she was laughing. Well, she decided not to speed anymore, and she did learn how to master that car.

It was time she learned the rules of the road and she finally got her license. The 1967 Volkswagen was air cooled with the motor and fan belt in the back of the car. The trunk was in the front. As a joke, she would ask guys if they could find a radiator cap for a 1967 Volkswagen; there was no radiator. Just like there is no such thing as blinker fluid. It didn't stop her from asking for it at the auto part stores just for fun.

Chapter 9

As Josey lifted the sheets from Ida Loren's bed, she held her breath. Ida looked up at her, "it's time to turn on your side Ida." Josey was lightheaded as she tugged at the lift sheet, gently turning Ida on her side.

Ida had only been a resident at the Pleasant View Medical Care Facility for a few days. She had transferred from the hospital after having both legs amputated above the knees. Josey hurried out of the room. As she stepped into the hall, she leaned against the wall closed her eyes and breathed a heavy sigh. "I can't do this," she cried, "I just can't."

After just one week on the unit Josey realized that what was taught in the nursing aid class was only the beginning. The registered nurse's words came back, "you have to give yourself at least six months to adjust to the things that you can only learn by being on the floor." She certainly was right, thought Josey. "I have only been here a week. Six months? I don't think so! I will try it but I don't think I can do this!?" she told herself.

The food carts came rolling down the hall with a "Thud, Thud, Thud" sound. As she pulled Ida's tray form the cart, she dreaded the argument she knew was about to take place.

"Mrs. Loren, your lunch is here," said Josey.

"I am not hungry," was Ida's response she knew too well.

"But you have to eat. Please try something. A person cannot live without food," Josey pleaded.

"I don't want to live Josey," said Ida with her back turned. "What is there to live for? I am going to die anyway," she added. Josey didn't know what to say. Just then the nurse came in with Ida's medication.

"How are you today Ida?" she asked. There was no response. Ida just stared out the window.

"Ida refuses to eat Nurse Hodge," said Josey.

"Well, that is her right," replied the nurse. "She can refuse'," she said as she turned and walked out of the room. Josey followed her.

"You mean to tell me that she can just refuse and just lay there and waste away?" Josey asked.

"I am afraid so Josey. We cannot force a patient to eat. It is against the law to force a resident. Ida is terminally ill and that is a terrible thing to have to live with," said Nurse Hodge.

On the wall above Ida's bed was a picture of her son that had passed away years before. She would tell loving stories about him. That night Josey tossed and turned; she could not sleep. "I have to keep trying. I have to find a way to at least get her to take in some kind of nourishment," she thought. She plumped her pillow behind her and sat up in bed.

"I cannot just let her do this to herself," Josey said to herself. Josey didn't know just how to handle this, but she knew she had to keep trying. Looking up, she whispered, "please help me with this one, it's a tuffy."

The next morning when the breakfast cart came Josey took Ida's tray and hurried to her room. In a cheery voice she whispered, "breakfast is here Ida."

Ida moaned, "I'm not hungry." Josey rolled Ida's bed into a sitting position.

"Well maybe you can humor me," Josey said with a smile. Ida looked up at her with soft brown eyes. "Just try to drink something for me Ida," Said Josey. Josey held the glass of milk to Ida's mouth as she sipped at it.

"That's all I can drink," said Ida.

"Well, you only drank half the glass," said Josey.

"Well, that is all I want," snapped Ida.

"Ok," said Josey, "I will leave you alone." Josey left the room thinking, "well half a glass is more than she did yesterday." I just have to keep trying. At ten o'clock the nourishment trays came, and Josey took a glass of milk and cup of Jello for Ida.

Josey bounced into Ida's room with a confident smile. "Ida, I have some Jello and milk for you. Everyone likes Jello," she said. Giving Ida a bite, she looked out the window and cheered, "oh look at that bird at the window." The birds were starting to find the feeder that the maintenance man had placed in front of Ida's window. Taking another bite of Jello, Ida stretched to see the blue bird that was hungrily pecking away.

She looked at Josey and smiled, "What a beautiful bird." "That Jello did taste pretty good," she added. Josey fed Ida the rest of the Jello and she drank half of the milk. As Ida took the last bite of Jello she Josey kissed her on the cheek.

"Now that's more like it. Maybe there will be something good on your lunch tray today," said Josey. As Josey rolled the head of her bed down, she noticed a tear in Ida's left eye. Ida smiled, turned her head, and closed her eyes.

Ida began to eat more each day. She started gaining weight and sitting up more. She began visiting with the other residents and sharing more stories about her beloved son. She also ate in the dining room every now and then. One day, while Josey was putting her to bed, Ida looked up at her and said, "thank you for making my life worth living." Tears ran down Josey's face as she hugged her. For nearly a year, Ida enjoyed her meals with Josey and the life itself with the other residents at Pleasant View before she died. Her and Josey laughed and cried and shared secrets.

The last days were comfortable ones for Ida with Josey by her side. However, for Josey, there were times that she felt like she couldn't take another day. Josey went on the work there for nearly ten years. Somehow the memories of the good days and the laughter she shared with residents were more powerful than the sadness. She helped bring more life to Ida and others like her. She wouldn't have it any other way.

Chapter 10

Josey would sit under the trees and write her stories. The cool breezes would relax her and send her thoughts soaring. With the hustle of the house chores, the television blaring, and the children playing her thoughts were all a jumble. She would go off by herself to just listen to the birds and rustle of the leaves to calm her nerves. She would watch the butterflies and the bees flying about. She could connect with nature. She would drift back into the world of nature and imagination. The calmness of getting away into her own world was soothing.

She would drift off into her own little cartoon world and imagine what life would be like in another place and another time. After a time, she would realize that she would have to go back to reality. Her own little vacation was over. Sitting on the porch she was relaxing and reading the newspaper. Here comes her little neighbor Angela.

"Know what? My mom painted my room. I have a picture of a pear in a tree on my wall and I have a picture of a butterfly too. I want Teresa to come over and see my new room. I have a new baby cousin her name is Courtney. She is so cute. She gots little hands. My Aunt

Linda let me hold her. My brother Ricky got to hold her too. Aunt Linda asked Jimmy if he wanted to hold her, but he wouldn't," she rambled on. "I hurt my knee because, I fell off my bike. I can go real fast on it. My mom said I could ride my bike anytime I want but I can't go past our street. Sometimes me and Ricky race and I can beat him sometimes. I want Sheila to go swimming with us tomorrow. My mom will take us to the pool, and we can go on one end," she went on and on.

"It's too deep on the other side of the pool. My mom got a sunburn last time we went swimming. She said she wasn't going to do that again. It hurt her to wear clothes. I don't get sunburns and my mom buys sunscreen now. My birthday is pretty soon. I want a Candyland game. My mom said I could have a party. I want all the neighbor kids to come. Can your kids come? My mom is going to get a cake and ice cream and we can play games. I am going to be eight. My dad's mad at our neighbors. Their dog keeps coming over in our yard. He chewed up our hose and boy our dad got mad." She just always kept going on and on. She couldn't be stopped until she was done with her thought.

The neighbor dogs name is Joey. He's a German dog. He's a puppy but he is big. Angela just kept talking about that dog. "I like to pet him. He always tries to lick my face. Yuk! I hate that. Me and the dog run around the yard. It's fun! If I throw a frisbee sometimes he catches it. He chewed it up too. One time he got one of my dad's shoes off the porch and my dad didn't know where it was. I found it by the road all chewed up. Now my dad don't leave his shoes on the porch no more. He had to get new shoes."

When she would sit and talk with Josey, she would just keep talking even if no one talked back to her, she just told story after story. "My mom's going to take me to get my hair cut today. I just want it cut a little. I want it to be long. My Aunt Bonnie's hair is real long. She has a hard time combing it. Sometimes she lets me brush it. It's real shiny and soft. I want my hair to look like that. My cousin got gum in her hair and she had to cut it. When I chew gum, I throw it away when I go to bed. You can't get long hair if you keep cutting it off. It's almost two o'clock. I think my mom wants me home by two o'clock so she can take me to the beauty shop. I better go so I won't be late. Bye, Josey," she finally ended.

"What a little magpie," thought Josey. She never got two words of the conversation in with her little neighbor, but Josey thought she was so cute as she jumped off the porch and got on her bike and went for home.

Josey enjoyed the kids coming up on her porch to talk to her. Josey can't remember talking so much when she was a girl growing up in Missouri. She didn't really like talking a lot. She spent a lot of time by herself. She had mostly brothers and they were annoying. They would take the heads off her dolls and chase her with them. She got tired of that and just stopped playing with dolls. She would climb trees to get away from them to be by herself. Her sister Helen didn't talk much either. She would just sit and play in the dirt. There was not a lot of toys just sticks and rocks. There were no pools, just mud holes to jump in when it rained.

Chapter 11

Josey has worked many jobs and sometimes she worked more than one full-time job at a time. She has done roofing, siding, waitressing, sewing, and landscaping. All sorts of jobs. She learned how to make a buck. Her children never went hungry or cold. They didn't always have the best, but they didn't need the best to be happy.

Josey cleaned, did laundry, and babysat for others. She made ends meet. Her children grew and went on their own and had their own families. Josey was left alone to her own memories, good and bad. Her children stayed close. She started renting rooms and sewing for other people. She rented to very different people and this became a big challenge. She was always up for a challenge, the bigger the better. It's not easy sharing your home with other people. The ups and downs, likes and dislikes can be tiresome.

To have others sharing your home is sometimes wild, sometimes wonderful, maddening, and crazy. All in all, there has to be some sort of stability. One chief among the Indians that will take charge. So many different ways of thinking can throw you on and off. A raging rollercoaster ride, staying at least three steps ahead. You have to be kind and rough at the same time to maintain stability. Set rules and be flexible.

Renters came and went. Some good, some bad. You cannot be afraid to face them. It's like a cartoon world that can get to the point of being out of control, but you have to reach out sometimes and put someone off the ride.

Jeff was a drinker. Boy that was a ride, but Josey had alcoholics in her family so this was not new to her. He started out being a good, kind fellow; like they always do. He came with no money, no clothes, and no place to go. She took him in until his next monthly check, got his clothes, and settled him in. The next month she started charging room and board.

No one cooks in Josey's kitchen but her. That was the pure hillbilly in her. A hillbilly's kitchen was their lone stomping ground. She would try to make different foods that all her renters liked. A hillbilly cook all the way; fried everything. She did all the cooking, cleaning, laundry, and yard work. Her trailer they lived in was small, but different. She called it her get acquainted house. She earned her money. She kept plenty of food, coffee, and snacks stocked up.

Sometimes there were three people besides Josey, sometimes four. She managed to keep the house clean and in somewhat order. The house ran smoothly most of the time. Josey told the guys they could make hamburgers at night if they got hungry. She bought boxes of hamburger patties that she kept in the freezer. One night she woke up to three-foot flames in her kitchen at the stove. The guys decided to cook a dozen burgers at once. She came running in the kitchen to see a huge flame over the big cast iron skillet. She threw a wet towel over it.

"Ok you shitheads," she yelled, "no more monkeys cooking in the kitchen. I do all the cooking from now on no matter what. There are snacks here, I will do all the shopping and cooking here. Stay out of my kitchen." She told them they could buy their own snacks and drink extra but no alcohol.

The rules got tougher to fit the crimes. There was no fighting allowed and she was the warden. Things went well most of the time. It was a learn as you go process. Most of the time everything went well. She needed their income. and they needed a place to live. She told them she was the only bitch in the house, and it stayed that way. If there was a dispute, they were to take it to her, and she would settle it. She was on her toes all the time, and it kept her strong.

The renters came and went but Josey paid the bills. Jeff stayed there for a long time. He did his share of shit, but it always got straightened out. Josey would tell him, "I have a breaking point and you never know when that is. Let's hope you never find out!"

He would hide whiskey in his jacket sometime and she knew it. When he was drinking whiskey, he was an ass. She told him he could drink a limited amount of beer sometimes unless he got stupid. He would still try to hide whiskey sometimes in his room, but she knew it.

One night Mike turned his stereo full blast. Josey said, "Ok Mike, if that's what you want to do." Josey had the fuse box, so she simply pulled the fuse to his room cutting off his power. That solved that and he didn't do that again. She tolerated a lot before she lashed out at the guys.'

After a time, Mike moved in with a girlfriend. When they split up, he came to Josey's door wanting to come back. Josey slammed the door in his face yelling, "shit too!" Jeff, of course, was still there. Still renters came and went. She never failed to get her rent and keep her bills paid.

Mitch was the son of Josey's good friends Sue and Marty. He had stayed here and there when he needed help getting on his feet. He would be helpful to Josey when he could.

Nancy called Josey one day and asked to move in. Josey knew she was a pastor's wife. Nancy's husband had passed away. Josey asked her if she used swear words.

Nancy said, "no, but I know you do."

Josey told her, "well, this is my house, and I will talk the way I want."

"That's fine with me," Nancy said, and she moved in. When she came to Josey's trailer she could walk. Eventually Nancy was bedridden, and Josey now takes care of her.

Since then, Jeff has moved out. He was being disrespectful to Josey and Nancy. Josey finally told him it was time for him to leave. He actually told her he didn't have to. Josey said, "I told you from the beginning that I was the only bitch in this house, and it stays that way. You never know when this bitch has had enough. Now, I have had enough!"

He had the nerve to tell her he was calling the cops. She told him go ahead because, she is the senior citizen there so get the hell out. He still refused. She smashed him against the wall and told him to leave or she would put him out. Well, he finally left.

Bonnie was a wonderful friend and renter, but she moved in and out several times. Josey misses her. She will always have a place in her home and in her heart.

Chapter 12

Josey had crazy, tiring times with renting. Her very good friend, Rod comes and goes. He helps her with the yard and the household. He has been like a guardian angel, always there when she needs him. She now has a room set up for her sewing business. She calls it "Bev's Sew What: the busines with an attitude". It has its ups and downs but is pretty stable. With fifty years of sewing experience, it all works out.

She also has a page on Facebook and gets many likes. She charges very little for her sewing. She has a customer appreciation wall that her customer's sign, it has gotten pretty full. Josey's puggle, Sally Mae has been with her almost 15 years and still going strong for her age. Her puppy a pug named Sally Kae keeps her busy. She keeps her strong and challenged. She is a handful but is learning more each day. Staying busy can keep you healthy and wise.

Josey's love life through the years has been a struggle too. Marriage is a wonderful thing if you can maintain it. It doesn't happen for her. She has enough love for her family and children and the life God gave her to keep things strong. Her hillbilly home life stays within her. Nature stays with her, floating butterflies, bee stings, and growing gardens, all God's plan.

Cupid shot her in the ass a few times until she realized something stung her. Until she learned how to dodge the arrows. But through all the trials of life, she is still full of love for her fellow man that shares the earth with her.

She still loves the growing vegetables, the tall trees, the sewing, the writing, and keeping the pace. The whole world is hers and everything that is in it. Just like the poem "IF" by Rudyard Kipling, you have to be strong and loving and you can make it through.

Josey has had cancer three times, lost a kidney, lost loved ones, and still life is important. Her friends and family, people in general, should love what they have, not what they don't.

Epilogue

Josey's favorite son, her only son Billy Lee passed away one hot July afternoon, leaving two sons and a daughter. His son Christopher has a son little Chris. Robert has a daughter, Amelia and Nicky has a son Logan. Billy's beautiful grandchildren.

Billy's son Robert also passed away shortly after him.

Josey's daughter Debbie has two daughters: Courtney and Claudia. Courtney has 4 children: Amelia, Jacob, Liam, and Luna. Claudia has a daughter, Aurora. Debbie's beautiful grandchildren. Debbie has also been an amazing and creative artist and a domestic engineer.

Sarah Jane Loberg has no children but is happy and healthy with her cat Mittens. She is a published writer. Her book "The Day Uncle Butch Cut the Cheese" is now on Amazon.

Lisa has three children: Elijah, Briana, and Ethan. Elijah has a daughter, Elayna and Briana has a son, Jaden. They were born one day apart. Lisa's beautiful grandchildren. Ethan is the illustrator for Sarah's book. Lisa is an apartment manager.

Sheila has three children, three daughters: Alexis, Ariana, and Alivia Belle. Sheila is a nurse in a hospital caring for the newborn babies.

Teresa has a son and a daughter, Madalyn Jo and Ford Henry. She is a family nurse practitioner and works in Urgent Care.

Josey's children stay close to her. She is proud of them. They have families of their own and live productive lives.

Josey's brothers Jim and Bobby have passed away. Jim's son David Swarbrick is a published writer. Her brother Wayne has had bouts with cancer and major surgeries. He is still going strong. Josey's brother Gordon is also a published writer. Josey's brother Ray lives in California. His wife had passed away. They have one daughter, Dawna. He calls Josey often.

Josey's good friend Rich has helped her a lot along the way.

The love of nature, family, and her experiences of all the good, the bad, and the ugly that she met along life's path gave her strength to go beyond what she thought was possible.

Bev Beck Titles Include:

 01: Benny At The Bop™
ISBN: 9781590953747

 02: The Acorn Nuts™
ISBN: 9781590953754

 03: The Birthday Present™
ISBN: 9781590953761

 04: The Hollers Bunch Goes to Lunch™
ISBN: 9781590953778

 05: Can You Just Imagine™
ISBN: 9781590953785

 07: The Curwood Acorns™
ISBN: 9781590951262

 08: Lonny Lemon™
ISBN: 9781648830143

 09: Josey's Hillbilly Heaven™
ISBN: 9781590954683

06: Title: Hillbilly Heaven™

Author: Bev Beck
Publisher: TotalRecall Publications
Paper Back: ISBN: 9781590954683
eBook: ISBN: 9781590954690
Publication Date: 2021

Hillbilly Heaven is based on a true story.

Josey grew up in the bountiful foothills of the Missouri Ozarks with her little brothers and sister. As her thoughts take her back to those hills, she will make you laugh. The secrets that these beautiful hills hold may startle you.

Josey is a strong-willed youngster that endures a lot of trials. Through memories and secrets she will reveal to you the tolerance and durability of what children can endure together when left without a choice.

True life can sometimes be more bizarre than any movie!

www.ingramcontent.com/pod-product-compliance
Lightning Source LLC
Chambersburg PA
CBHW050501110726
47899CB00003B/1037